FART SQUAD

BLAST FROM THE PAST

CHAPTER ONE

"Wakey, wakey, Mr. Stonkadopolis," a voice whispered.

Darren Stonkadopolis could hardly open his eyes. "Who's that?" he mumbled before reaching down the back of his pants to scratch himself. He scratched and scratched and furiously scratched some more, but instead of calming the raging itch in his butt, he only made things worse.

"It is I, Harold Buttz, *Senior*. Owner of the Buttz Factory, Buttz Industries, Buttz Bakery, Buttz Office Supply, Buttz Savings and Loan, and two-thirds of everything else in Buttzville. Now WAKE UP, son! We've no time to waste!"

Darren's eyes popped wide open. "Whoa!" he shouted, realizing Harold Buttz's face was hovering only an inch from his own. There was just enough light to make out his super-thick sideburns and his black fedora, with a long turquoise peacock feather sticking out from the side.

Where am I? Darren wondered. *And what's Harold Buttz, the richest man in all of Buttzville, doing here?*

Darren quickly got up from the cot he'd been lying on. Now he could see that the rest of the Squad was asleep in cots next to his. But how did they all get there in the first place?

"I must apologize for my men's slightly aggressive tactics," Mr. Buttz said.

With that, the nightmarish details of the

last twelve hours all came flooding back to Darren. The army of scary-looking men in black suits and sunglasses sneaking up on them. The frenzied, fart-powered retaliation. And finally, a stabbing feeling that came from behind and then: darkness.

"Slightly?" Darren squawked. "They took us down with tranquilizer darts!"

"Well, that's why I'm apologizing!" Buttz barked. "But I had to ensure your arrival by any means necessary. I need you and your friends to complete the most important mission in the history of Buttzville."

"Mission?" Darren was still a little woozy. "What kind of mission? And how do you know who I am, anyway?"

"How do I know?" Mr. Buttz

snorted. "I'm Harold R. Buttz, son. I know everything."

"Dude..." Juan-Carlos Finkelstein sat up drowsily in his cot. "Where are we?" Normally, he would have chimed in with a bad joke, but he was focused on relieving his own raging itch by dragging himself across the floor in a seated position, like a Chihuahua that had just eaten chili.

"I, too, am baffled by this dim and unfamiliar location," Walter Turnip, the heaviest and most well-spoken Fart Squad member, added as he raked his behind with the fork he kept with him at all times in case of unexpected food opportunities.

"This is all so inappropriate." Tina Heiney sighed. She may have looked like an adorable little princess, but the stink of her silent-but-deadly farts was lethal.

"Linda!" Mr. Buttz shouted into the darkness. "Our young heroes are finally awake. Lights on!"

A loud *ker-chunk* echoed overhead as blinding floodlights suddenly whirred to life.

Shielding his eyes from the bright lights, Darren looked around, and his mind was officially blown.

The stone walls of the room stretched as far and as high as five school auditoriums. Half of the enormous hall looked like it was from the future, and the other half looked like it was hundreds of years old—like a medieval castle.

Darren recognized the weapons hanging all over the walls from pictures he'd seen in Mr. Krustenshortz's history class. But then, in between those old weapons, there were twenty-foot-high HDTV screens and massive supercomputers made of space-age plastic and glass. Men and women in white coats were sitting at big touch-screen consoles that looked like iPads for giants. One of those women, Darren assumed, was named Linda.

"Impressive, isn't it?" Mr. Buttz boasted, spreading his arms wide. "I had the entire complex modeled after Castle

Buttz, my family's medieval castle in Scotland. It's the largest collection of medieval weaponry in the world. It's also the finest collection of cutting-edge technology in the world. Yes, Bruce Wayne may have his Batcave, but this, my young friends... this is the Buttz-cave!"

For one rare moment, even Juan-Carlos was speechless.

"Now, come," Buttz said, clapping his hands to make sure the Squad was fully awake. "We must get to the tower immediately to begin the mission."

Tina looked very confused. "What tower?"

"Yeah, and what

mission?" Darren asked again.

"You're going to save our entire town from the Itch," Mr. Buttz declared.

"The *entire* town?" Juan-Carlos asked.

"Linda!" Mr. Buttz shouted. "Bring up the local news onscreen. Show them what's happening aboveground."

The WBRP News suddenly came up on every screen in the Buttz-cave. It was a helicopter shot from high over

Buttzville, showing a line of desperately itchy citizens that stretched all the way from the Buttzville Pharmacy through to the center of town. All the townspeople had their hands jammed down the backs of their pants, scratching wildly at their backsides. The news crawl read:

"BUTTZVILLE STRICKEN WITH POSTERIOR ITCH . . . TOWN IN DESPERATE NEED OF OINTMENT."

"Posterior itch . . . ?" Juan-Carlos stared up at the screen.

"Butt itch," Darren whispered in shock. "The whole town has butt itch!

Just like Harry. . . ."

"Indeed," Mr. Buttz said gravely. "Just like my son, Harry, Jr., and every other Buttz throughout history. The town has been stricken with the Buttz family curse. We can't afford to waste another minute. Come!" He hurried them along. "You'll be briefed for the mission on the way to the tower."

"Briefed?" Juan cracked a goofy half smile. "But I'm already wearing underwear." Even in a crisis, he couldn't resist a terrible pun. "Get it?" he added. "Because briefs is another word for—"

"Not *now*, Juan," Tina huffed.

"Yes, not now, Juan!" Mr. Buttz shouted. "Everyone into the Buttz-mobile!" He trotted over to a black, six-seat golf cart parked against the wall, and hopped into the driver's seat.

"*That's* the Buttz-mobile?" Juan chuckled. "Really?"

"That it is," Buttz said. "I've given the motor a few modifications, though. All aboard!"

The Squad climbed into their seats. When Mr. Buttz stepped on the gas, the Buttz-mobile took off like a rocket.

CHAPTER TWO

The Buttz-mobile raced down the long, stone tunnels of the Buttz-cave, as Mr. Buttz briefed them for their mission.

"Ah, that infernal Itch!" he shouted over the whir of the golf cart's motor. "My family has been cursed with it since the Middle

Ages, you see! That's why my ancestor, the brilliant alchemist Psoracious Buttz, tried to create a cure. He forged a powerful butt scratcher that helped the family scratch the Itch away."

"The Golden Butt Scratcher!" Darren blurted out. "But I thought it was forged by Scabious Buttz right here in Buttzville?"

Buttz shook his head. "Not exactly, young

man. You've probably noticed by now that we Buttzes are a gentle sort, so when poor Scabious, who by all accounts was a batty old man, started to believe he invented the Scratcher, no one had the heart to correct him. It's an open family secret that Psorious Buttz, a medieval Scotsman, was the actual genius behind it all."

Why would anyone bother taking credit for something so problematic? Darren wondered. Sure, the Scratcher worked, up to a point, but its design system was so flawed, it wasn't anything to brag about. The Scratcher operated by collecting all the itches, but as soon as it couldn't contain them anymore, it burst like a dam, unleashing all the stored-up itch on anyone unlucky enough to be within range.

The effect was brutal. Lives came to a halt, as no one could concentrate on anything besides alleviating themselves. Townspeople were so frightened, they finally put an end to it all by stealing the Scratcher from Scabious and burying it deep in a swamp, in the hopes that no one would ever find it again. The only problem was, someone did find it.

Harry Buttz II. Or, as many liked to call him, Number Two.

A few months ago, Harry II had an itch the likes of which he'd never experienced before. He tried every remedy he could think of, but none of them brought him any relief. Convinced there was only one solution, he dug up the Scratcher and tested it out.

It took the full gaseous powers of the Fart Squad to wrest the Scratcher from Harry's grubby hands and destroy it before it wreaked havoc again. At least, that was Darren's intention. But now he realized . . .

"I wasn't *saving* the town by destroying the Scratcher; it was just the opposite. When I blew that thing to bits, I must have spread its collected itch across Buttzville!

"But that was months ago," Tina shouted over the motor. "How come everyone just started itching now?"

"The incubation period," Buttz explained. "It was just a few itchy rats in the sewers at first, but it finally spread to the entire town. My crack team of scientists has been

working on the problem for months."

"A *crack* team?" Juan-Carlos giggled. "So I guess they're all plumbers, right? You know, 'cause when plumbers bend down, you can always see their—"

"NOT NOW, JUAN!" the entire Buttz-mobile hollered.

"But there must be some kind of cure," Darren hoped. "Some kind of antidote that can stop all the itching?"

"I'm afraid not," Mr. Buttz replied. "My

scientists have tried everything, but to no avail. Once that scratcher exploded over Buttzville, we were all doomed."

"Then it's true," Darren said, feeling a sharp pang of guilt in his belly. "The Itch is all my fault."

"Don't be ridiculous!" Buttz said. "I told you, my family is to blame. If it weren't for that infernal scratcher, none of this would have happened. That's why we must erase the Scratcher from history."

"Erase it?" Darren asked.

"Yes," Mr. Buttz said. "If we erase the Scratcher from history, then there'd be nothing for my foolish son to dig up, and nothing for you to blow up. If there'd never been a Scratcher, then Buttzville never would have gotten the Itch in the first place."

"Um . . . yeah," Tina said, dubiously. "But just how exactly do we erase it from history?"

"By going back in time, of course," Buttz replied.

The Fart Squad went silent. For the first time, it occurred to Darren that Mr. Buttz might be completely insane.

"What exactly do you mean by 'back in time'?" Walter asked.

"I mean, you need to go back to the sixteenth century and destroy that Scratcher."

"The sixteenth century!?"

"Yes, my lad. Back to the *original* Castle Buttz in Tusheeburgh, Scotland. Back then, it was called the Royal Butt Scratcher, and it was kept under strict guard by the great and mighty Knights of Tushée."

Juan-Carlos's face turned visibly red as he tried not to crack up. "Wait ... the Knights of *Tushie*?"

"It's pronounced Tu-*shay*!" Buttz barked. "The Knights of Tush-*ée*, not tushie! And believe me, you won't be laughing when you meet them. Those knights stopped at nothing to protect the Royal Butt Scratcher. Why do you think I've recruited you all for this mission? You're the only ones in Buttzville who can possibly defeat the Knights of Tushée. The only ones who can possibly get to that scratcher and destroy it!"

"Sir, if I may?" Walter raised his hand.

"Yes, the round one in the back," Buttz said, calling on Walter.

"Thank you," Walter said. "The part about

destroying the Scratcher certainly seems within our powers. But the part about traveling back through time . . . I do not believe that any amount of superpowered flatulence can actually disrupt the space-time continuum."

"Oh, you think you can't fart your way back in time?" Buttz asked.

"It seems unlikely," Walter replied.

"Well then, let me introduce you . . . to *Turbo Taco*."

CHAPTER THREE

Mr. Buttz slammed on the brakes of the Buttz-mobile, and it came to a screeching halt in front of a huge, empty silo.

"We've reached the tower," he announced. "I'll need you all to run to the large X, please."

The Fart Squad stepped out of the car and rushed across the black tarmac to the white, painted X in the center of the cavernous tower. It looked kind of like a landing pad for a helicopter, or a launching pad for a rocket, but there wasn't a rocket in sight. Just a woman with black, frizzy hair, in a white lab coat, holding out a neon-green backpack.

She handed the backpack to Mr. Buttz, and pulled two large metal clips from her lab coat pocket. She pinned her nostrils shut with one of the clips and handed Mr. Buttz the other.

"Thank you, Linda," he said. "Now, listen closely," he told the Squad. "Whatever happens, *do not lose* this backpack. Be *extremely*

careful with it. The contents are your only way back in time, and your only way home. For inside this backpack, there is more gaseous power than mankind's digestive systems have ever known...."

He put on his nose clip and unzipped the bag. White smoke began billowing from inside, and Darren could immediately smell a truly foul odor that made his stomach twitch. The stench reminded him of the greasy, radioactive burritos that gave the Fart Squad their powers. But this was a whole other level of stink.

Mr. Buttz reached into the bag and pulled out a small bottle that glowed bright green. Smoke billowed out from under the cork top. The bottle had a small label on it with two backward triangles, like the rewind symbol on a video player. It was sandwiched in a thin, yellow neoprene case, making it look kind of

like a sizzling, radioac-
tive, hard-shell taco.

"Behold!" Mr. Buttz
shouted, holding the
bottle high. "Turbo
Taco! A time-travel elixir
designed specifically for
your unique digestive tal-
ents! One gulp of this will turn
your superpowered farts into *turbo*-powered
farts."

"Turbo?" Juan-Carlos clamped his nose
shut with his fingertips. "More like *turd*-o."
He raised his free hand. "Come on, someone
give me five for that one."

"I do feel that was deserving of five," Walter admitted, quickly giving Juan-Carlos a
high five.

"But what is it?" Darren asked, eyeing
the smoking bottle suspiciously.

"Oh, it would take hours to explain the specifics," Buttz said. "But to put it simply, we took every kind of bean known to man, distilled the mixture down to a hyper-flatulent, liquid essence, and ran it through a nuclear fission reactor over two hundred million times. Then we added tortilla chips. This formula will provide you with the exact amount of internal combustion necessary to blast you all the way back to the original Castle Buttz in Tusheeburgh, Scotland . . . in the year 1502." He turned to Walter. "You think you can't fart your way back in time, my round friend? Well, prepare to be amazed. . . ." He handed the smoking bottle to Walter.

Walter examined the bottle

and took a big whiff. "Hmm. I find the aroma repellent yet enticing. Perhaps a taste test is in order. I haven't eaten since breakfast." He tugged out the cork and hungrily brought the bottle closer to his mouth.

"Wait a minute, Walter!" Darren warned. "We don't even know what's going to happen if we drink that stuff."

But it was too late. One drop of the glowing, green liquid hit Walter's tongue . . .

And Walter went turbo.

A huge plume of white smoke shot out from his butt, as he blasted off into the air. The Turbo Taco was a million times more powerful than their radioactive burritos, and it sent him spinning wildly toward the roof of the tower, bouncing off the stone walls like a helium balloon that had just been pricked.

"No!" Buttz shouted up to Walter. "I said *prepare* to be amazed! I haven't given you all your instructions yet!"

"Well, perhaps now would be a good time!" Walter shouted back from the roof of the tower, trying in vain to steer his turbo-toots.

"You don't understand," Buttz said. "Once you drink Turbo Taco, you only have four minutes to make the time jump!"

"Or what happens?" Darren asked.

"That's not important right now," Buttz replied.

"No, tell us what happens," Tina insisted.

"It's called Reverse Diarrhea. It's very difficult to explain."

"*Reverse* Diarrhea?" Juan-Carlos squawked. "How would that even work?"

"You don't want to know!" Buttz barked. "So I suggest you activate the time jump!"

"Walter, drop the bottle down here!" Darren ordered.

Walter dropped the bottle and Darren made the catch. Most of the Turbo Taco had splattered all over the tower when Walter had taken off. There was just enough at the bottom for Darren, Tina, and Juan-Carlos to get a drop on their tongues. But one drop was all it took. . . .

Darren's stomach suddenly felt like a toaster that was warming up too quickly. Then it moved right past that phase into microwave territory, and the next thing he knew, there was a full-on thermonuclear war going on in his lower intestine.

"I'm okay," he called out, gripping his

gut, trying to think non-gaseous thoughts. "Everything is A.O.—*uh-oh* . . ." He dropped down on the floor like he was getting ready to do push-ups. "Everyone back away!" he hollered. "I don't think I can clench this one!"

He tried like crazy to clench his butt, but it was no use. He was more than used to firing off heated fart missiles, but this time a full-fledged lightning bolt escaped his behind and ignited Walter's fart stream, creating a king-size fireball in the middle of the silo. Everyone ducked down as the biggest lighted fart in history went up in flames.

Tina snatched the all-important green backpack from Mr. Buttz and hoisted it on her shoulders. "Just tell us how to activate the jump," she demanded.

"Someone needs to pull the index digit," Buttz said.

"In *English,* please." Tina sighed.

"Oh, for heaven's sake, Tina. Someone needs to pull your pointer!" Walter called down.

Despite all the impending doom, Juan-Carlos couldn't help grinning. "Seriously? That's how you activate the jump?"

"We tried to keep it simple," Buttz said.

"Fine!" Tina groaned. She turned to Juan-Carlos, held out her finger, and said what had to be said. "Juan . . . have at it."

Juan reached for Tina's finger when an earthshaking, megabomb suddenly exploded beneath their feet, catapulting Juan, Tina, and Darren toward Walter.

"Okay, that one was me!" Juan raised his hand to take credit for the turbo-powered fart grenade, as they were flung wildly through the air.

"Walter, a little help!" Darren hollered, reaching for Walter's hand. Walter steered

himself closer, and the entire Fart Squad managed to grab one another's hands, forming a circle in the air, riding on the wind of Walter's fart stream.

"Everyone grab a finger and pull," Darren ordered. "Ready? One . . . two . . . three . . ."

"PULL MY FINGER!" they shouted in unison.

Suddenly, they all had Walter's power times a thousand. Clouds of turbo gas spewed from their butts, spinning them in faster and faster circles, creating a massive fart-nado in the center of the tower.

Mr. Buttz and Linda ran to the doorway to get clear of the cyclone. But Darren heard a little voice calling out from the other side of the tower. . . .

"Hey!" the voice hollered. "What's going on in here?"

Darren recognized the whiney little voice instantly.

Harry Buttz, Jr., the biggest baby in all of Buttzville.

And he wasn't alone. He had the B.O. twins with him.

Bertha and

Oscar Scroggy were their names, and never, ever bathing was their game. They'd been held back in school so many times, they were probably old enough to graduate college by now. They were at least twice the size of everyone else, and twice as mean, but they pretty much followed Harry wherever he went, doing his bidding, as long as he kept buying them the latest video games.

Now they were following him straight toward the ungodly stench of the raging fartnado. Not that they would have noticed an ungodly stench given their chronic refusal to shower.

Harry ran toward the swarming fart cloud, looking up in awe, as the wind blew his hair back.

"Back away, Junior!" Mr. Buttz shouted from all the way across the tower. "You need to get clear of the tailwind!"

"What?" Harry called out.

"The tailwind!" Buttz shouted. "It can take you back with . . ."

But that was the last thing Darren heard. He kept spinning and spinning, faster and faster, till all he could see was a blur of shining stars and colored lights.

Then he felt the giant foot of Father Time kick him right in the butt, and he blasted off into nowhere. . . .

CHAPTER FOUR

Darren's eyes fluttered open. His face was lying flat against a cold stone floor. It felt like he was waking up in the Buttzcave all over again. He saw Walter, Tina, and Juan-Carlos lying next to him, but this time, he felt a brisk wind blowing on his sore backside. He could hear the wind howling over his head.

"Dude," Juan-Carlos grunted, sitting up on the floor. "Did anyone else just feel the world's biggest kick in the tush?"

"Affirmative," Walter replied, grimacing

as he rubbed his behind. He rolled left and right a few times until he got enough momentum to lift his rotund body back to its feet.

"Hey . . ." Tina looked around at the familiar stone walls. "Are we still in the Buttz-cave? Oh my god, did we just drink that nasty Turbo Taco for *nothing*?"

"HALT!" a deep voice growled. "Who goes there?"

The Fart Squad snapped to attention. When Darren looked across the vast stone hall, he was sure he was dreaming.... There were five towering knights in shiny suits of armor, all lined up atop a tall, marble staircase. They had huge, gleaming weapons cocked and ready for battle. Behind them was a golden throne adorned with rubies and emeralds. A big block of stone sat near the throne, holding a metal object that stuck out like the hilt of a sword. It looked just like the handle of the Golden Butt Scratcher. Only it wasn't golden. At least . . . not yet.

Could it be? *The Royal Butt Scratcher?*

"Guys," Juan-Carlos croaked. "I don't think this is the Buttz-cave."

"How *dare* you let the royal Buttz name fall from your lowly lips!" a bearded knight snarled with a thick Scottish accent. "Tell me, bandit, just how did you and your cunning team of dwarves get into the throne room?"

"Dwarves?" Tina crossed her arms, indignantly. "We're not dwarves."

"Tina," Darren whispered through clenched teeth. "Let's not give the knights any attitude, m'kay?"

"Not dwarves, ay?" The bearded knight came slowly down the marble stairs, advancing toward them with his sword held high. "Well, you'll surely *be* dwarves once we cut you down to size. Thought you could invade Castle Buttz, did you? Thought you could sneak in here and steal the Royal Butt Scratcher? Well . . . 'tis a mistake ye shall pay for with your lives. Knights of Tushée . . . ATTACK!"

"Wait!" Darren thrust out his palm.

For some reason, the knights actually waited.

"Speak," the bearded knight said. "We are honorable knights. Methinks the masked dwarf hath some final words," he announced.

"Okay," Darren said. "First of all, we're not bandits or dwarves. And second of all, we didn't come here to steal the Royal Butt Scratcher."

"Is that so?" the knight said, dubiously.

"It is," Darren replied. "We didn't come to steal it. We came to *destroy* it. Fart Squad . . . ATTACK!"

Darren whirled around and aimed his turbo-powered butt at the knight's broadsword, as Walter crouched down for a takeoff.

The Knights of Tushée let out a warning yell as they charged....

But all five knights suddenly passed out cold, like those fainting goats on YouTube. Their heavy armor crashed to the stone floor with a deafening clatter.

Darren was totally confused for a second, until he looked behind him and saw the sly smile on Tina's face.

"I already attacked," she said, examining her pink nail polish. "I'd been holding that one in since the Buttz-cave."

Apparently, her turbo-powered, silent-but-deadly farts could take down all the Knights of Tushée in one fell toot.

"Nice one, T." Juan-Carlos grinned. "Okay, we've got to work fast before they wake up. Let's destroy that butt scratcher and head back home before they even know what hit 'em!"

CHAPTER FIVE

Juan-Carlos raced up the marble stairs to the block of stone that held the Royal Butt Scratcher. He grabbed the Scratcher's handle to pull it from the stone holder, but for some reason, it was stuck. He wrapped both hands around the handle and tugged again, but no luck.

"Darren, a little help here?" His face was turning red from the strain of tugging on the darned thing.

"Guys, hurry," Tina said. "They're gonna wake up."

"Yeah, let's do this!" Darren raced up the stairs with Tina and Walter and grabbed the Scratcher with Juan-Carlos. "On three. Ready? One, two, *ugggh*." Even with both of them pulling, it was useless. It was like the Scratcher was superglued inside the stone.

"Darren, just blow the whole stone up with your butt," Tina suggested.

"Tina, it's a block of solid rock," Darren said. "I can't just fart my way through a mountain, you know."

"If I might interject at this juncture," Walter said. "Considering the sizable bolt of lightning you were able to emit after ingesting the Turbo Taco, it is not entirely unreasonable for Tina to posit the theory that you might in fact be able to . . . um . . . how did you put it, Tina?"

"Blow it up with his butt," Tina said.

"Precisely," Walter said.

"All right, all right," Darren agreed. "Juan, let go. I'm gonna give it a try."

But just as Juan was about to let go, a scornful laugh came from the bottom of the stairs.

"You fool…" The bearded knight laughed. All the knights had woken from their temporary fart daze and were raising their swords high again. "You thought you could pull the Scratcher from the stone? Know you *nothing* of the Royal Butt Scratcher?"

"I mean . . . I know a little," Juan-Carlos offered, meekly.

"Then you should know that only a pureblooded Buttz can pull the Scratcher from the stone! Castle Buttz has been without a king for many moons, but when the rightful king arrives, he shall pulleth the Scratcher from the stone, scratch his royal buttocks, and take his place on the golden throne. And you, bandit . . ." He pointed his sword directly at Juan-Carlos. "You are most definitely *not* a pure-blooded Buttz."

The knights began to climb the stairs.

"Okay, don't take another step," Juan-Carlos warned them. "You'll seriously regret it."

"We shan't fall for that ploy again, you little—"

A massive fart-splosion blew the knights flat off their feet. They went tumbling back down the stairs like five armored Humpty Dumpties, their heavy swords skittering across the floor.

"I tried to warn you." Juan-Carlos shrugged. He turned back to the Squad with a cocky smile. "I let that one rip, like, right after we got here," he said, marveling at the extended delay on his turbo-powered time-bomb toots. "Dudes, is it just me, or are these knights way less scary than Mr. Buttz made it sound? I thought there'd be, like, fifty of them or something."

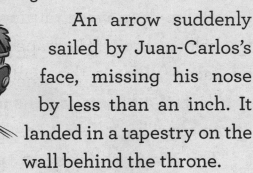

An arrow suddenly sailed by Juan-Carlos's face, missing his nose by less than an inch. It landed in a tapestry on the wall behind the throne. Juan-Carlos's eyes darted across the throne room just in time to see ten more knights pouring in, loading ten more arrows onto bulky crossbows. One of the knights was as tall as three Tinas and as wide as three Walters. His armored boots shook the floor with every monstrous step.

"My god!" the giant knight bellowed, his deep voice rattling the jewels on the golden throne. He draped his elbow over his face. "What is that foulest of odors? It smells as if a thousand hens laid a thousand rotten eggs!"

"The odor is but one in their arsenal of mysterious weapons!" the bearded knight warned, climbing back to his feet. "Knights of Tushée, with your helmets closed their vicious odors can't hurt us!"

The knights all raised their swords and drew back their crossbows.

Fifteen against four. Sixteen, if you counted the giant knight twice. This was not looking good. But when had that ever stopped the Squad before?

"Fart Squad," Darren said, clenching his fists and loosening his butt cheeks. "Prepare for battle."

Walter farted himself to the castle's vaulted ceiling, readying for an aerial assault.

"What—what?" the giant knight bellowed from inside his helmet as he watched Walter rise. "What wicked magic is this? They're not just dwarf bandits. They're dwarf bandit wizards!"

"That's right," Juan-Carlos said, stepping forward and puffing out his skinny chest. "We *are* wizards. And we practice in the Dark Farts."

"Rude!" the giant growled, raising his fist to the ceiling. "Such language in the throne room? Now they hath crossed the line. Knights of Tushée…ATTAAAAAAAACK!"

"Fart Squad!" Darren hollered. "ATTA-AAAAAAACK!"

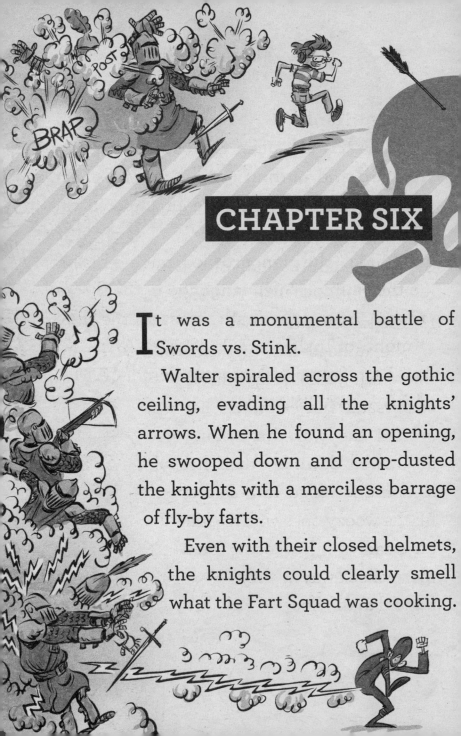

CHAPTER SIX

It was a monumental battle of Swords vs. Stink.

Walter spiraled across the gothic ceiling, evading all the knights' arrows. When he found an opening, he swooped down and crop-dusted the knights with a merciless barrage of fly-by farts.

Even with their closed helmets, the knights could clearly smell what the Fart Squad was cooking.

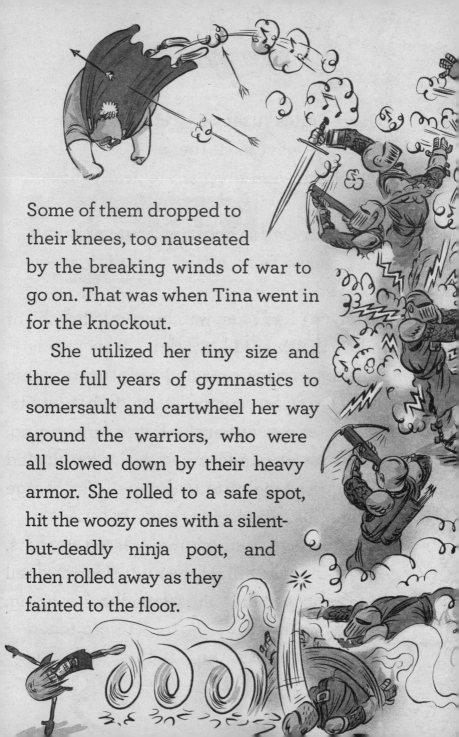

Some of them dropped to their knees, too nauseated by the breaking winds of war to go on. That was when Tina went in for the knockout.

She utilized her tiny size and three full years of gymnastics to somersault and cartwheel her way around the warriors, who were all slowed down by their heavy armor. She rolled to a safe spot, hit the woozy ones with a silent-but-deadly ninja poot, and then rolled away as they fainted to the floor.

Juan-Carlos used his lanky frame to slither his way past the swipes of their broadswords, and drop strategically placed fart bombs.

But Juan-Carlos and Tina could only pull it off because Darren was providing excellent cover.

If anyone had been watching through the window, they would have thought there was a lightning storm going on inside the throne room. Darren was firing off white-hot butt lightning at a feverish pace. It was leaving charred black marks all over the knights' armor, and all over the walls.

When he wasn't ducking behind the throne to avoid their arrows, Darren would pop out and take aim at the knights' swords and crossbows, hitting more than a few with his thunderous *blatts*. High-pitched yelps followed as the knights' weapons melted in their hands.

The battle might have gone on for hours. Maybe even days. But everything changed when Darren heard that voice again. That bratty little voice . . .

"Where's my daddy?" the voice whined from the hall. "And what's all that racket in there?"

It couldn't be. There was no way. Darren ducked down behind the golden throne and listened again.

"Daddy . . . ?" the voice called out again. "Daddy, where are you? I just had the weirdest dream. I dreamed I got caught in the world's smelliest tornado, and then a giant foot kicked me in the butt!"

It was most definitely Harry, Jr. *But what on earth was Harry, Jr. doing in 1502?*

Darren was totally baffled. But then he remembered the last thing he'd heard in the

Buttz-cave, right before the time jump. Mr. Buttz had been yelling something at Harry about a "tailwind," but Darren had only heard part of what he'd said:

"It can take you back with . . . ," he'd said.

But now Darren understood the rest of that sentence. *It can take you back with them.* That's what Mr. Buttz had been trying to tell Harry. The Squad's tailwind had swept Harry back in time, too! He must have landed in one of the other rooms in the castle.

Harry burst in through the backdoor of the throne room like he owned the place. Because he thought he *did* own the place. The Buttz-cave had been modeled on Castle Buttz, after all. He thought he was still at home.

"Daddy . . . ?" Harry stepped up next to the throne, and his jaw dropped wide

open as he peered
down the marble stairs.
He took in the sight of
fifteen knights with
swords and cross-
bows, and quickly
surmised that he was
not, in fact, home. Not
by a long shot.

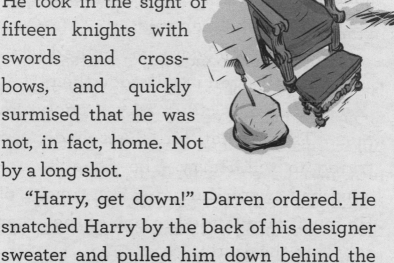

"Harry, get down!" Darren ordered. He snatched Harry by the back of his designer sweater and pulled him down behind the throne just before an arrow almost hit him right between the eyes.

"Oh, *I* get it . . ." Harry whispered to himself. "The smelly tornado wasn't the dream. *This* is the dream. The tornado must have made me bump my head, and now I'm dreaming. It's just like *The Wizard of Oz!*"

"No," Darren assured him. "This is not

The Wizard of Oz. You caught the tailwind of the booster farts that sent us back in time, and now you're in Tusheeburgh, Scotland, in the year 1502."

"Oh, yeah, that sounds *way* more realistic." Harry groaned, rolling his eyes. "No, this is *totally* my dream. I've had this one a million times. This is the one where the Buttz-cave turns into the *real* Castle Buttz, and there are real knights everywhere, and I get to run around the castle as much as I want, and eat whatever I want, and ... and ... my butt never itches ..." His eyes drifted to the Scratcher in the stone, and a huge smile broke out on his face. "See?" he whispered to himself. "It's my dream. And in my dream, I get to have my butt scratcher back!" He crawled out from behind the throne.

"Harry, no!" Darren reached for him, but Harry was already crawling his way to the stone.

Harry reached up for the Scratcher and pulled it right from the stone without a hint of effort. Then he used it to give his butt a quick scratch.

"Knights of Tushée, HOLD!" The bearded knight gave the signal to cease fire. He flipped his helmet open and gazed at Harry in awe. "See how the boy wields the Royal Scratcher?" he gasped. "See how he pulled it from the stone?"

All the knights gasped at once.

"And see how he scratcheth his buttocks!" the giant knight added.

Now all eyes had turned to Harry, who'd frozen in place with the Scratcher still stuck down his pants.

"Only a pure-blooded Buttz would have the power to pull the Scratcher from the stone!" the bearded knight proclaimed. "The rightful king of Tusheeburgh hath arrived! He hath finally arrived!"

The knights dropped down on one knee and bowed to Harry.

"All hail King…" The giant knight stopped short and lowered his voice. "Boy … what is thy name?"

"Harry," he replied.

"All hail King Harry!" the giant shouted.

"The rightful King of Tusheeburgh!"

"ALL HAIL KING HARRY!" the chorus of knights agreed.

"See, I *told* you," Harry whispered to Darren. "I have this dream, like, every day."

One of the knights pulled a ram's horn from his belt and blew a deafening signal that echoed through the entire castle, and

quite possibly through all of Tusheeburgh. A moment more and a horn blew a loud reply from within the castle. The next thing Darren knew, a full *stampede* of knights came piling into the throne room.

"Okay, this is more what I pictured," Juan-Carlos murmured, slowly backing up against the wall. "Dudes, this whole situation here is very, very bad."

"Darren," Tina called out. "The Scratcher's out of the stone. Take the shot and we can still get out of here!"

"Methinks the king is in peril!" the giant shouted. "We must protect the king!"

"WE MUST PROTECT THE KING!" the chorus of knights echoed, as they leaped to form a circle around Harry and his precious butt scratcher.

"My lord," the bearded knight said to Harry, "this dastardly team of dwarf bandit wizards attempted to invade Castle Buttz and destroy your Royal Scratcher. What shall be their punishment?"

"Hmmmmmmm," Harry wondered aloud. Darren couldn't see him behind the wall of knights, but he could practically hear the spoiled brat grinning from ear to ear. "Punishment, punishment, let me think . . ."

Just then, two very late guests arrived to Harry's coronation.

Bertha and Oscar Scroggy lumbered in, flushed, sweaty, and gasping for breath. They looked like two giant Christmas hams on legs. Apparently, the tailwind had swept them up, too. They really did follow Harry anywhere he went. Even if it was 1502.

"Where have you been?" Bertha grunted.

"Yeah, we looked everywhere for you, Number Two," Oscar huffed.

"Don't *call* me that!" Harry snapped,

moving the knights aside so he could point his scratcher at the twins like a royal scepter.

Now, for the first time in his life, he wasn't Harry Buttz II, and so that nickname finally didn't apply. Now he was the one and only king of Tusheeburgh.

Harry whirled back around and pointed his scratcher-scepter at Darren. "I have decided their punishment!"

"Yes, my lord?" said the bearded knight.

"Do I have a dungeon?" Harry double-checked.

"Yes, of course, my lord."

"Heck, yeah, I do!" the little king crowed. "Well, I sentence them to the dungeon! For, like, a *thousand* years!"

"You heard your king! Seize them!"

The army of knights began closing in on the Squad.

Fifty to four. This was one battle Darren knew they couldn't win.

"Fart Squad!" he hollered. "RETREAT!"

"Window!" Walter yelped. "It's the only way out." They raced to the arched window, praying Walter still had enough gas left after a 500-year trip through time, followed by a full-blown battle.

Walter quickly grabbed hold of Tina, who grabbed hold of Darren, who grabbed hold of Juan-Carlos, and they sailed into the wind right before the giant knight took a swipe at Darren's legs with his broadsword.

And, with just a few feet out from the window . . .

Walter's turbo stream suddenly narrowed to a wisp of smoke. Then just a few putts of smoke . . .

And then nothing.

"I believe I have just run out of gas," Walter announced.

"Yeah, we got that, Walter," Juan-Carlos said, as they slowly fell into a nosedive.

A thirty-foot-wide moat surrounded the entire castle. Darren could see the ridged backs of the snapping crocodiles that floated through the moat's murky water and eagerly awaited an afternoon snack.

"Tina, hit 'em with an S.B.D.!" he shouted

against the wind, "and prepare for impact!"

Tina squeezed one out, and the crocs, possessing a sense of smell far superior to humans, took one whiff and turned into sleeping logs, just as the Fart Squad took the plunge into the dark-brown soup.

When Darren popped his head back out of the water, there were guards surrounding the entire moat.

King Harry leaned out of his throne-room window with Bertha and Oscar on either side of him. He grinned at the washed-up heroes, and waved his scratcher-scepter at them like he was waving good-bye.

CHAPTER SEVEN

Yes, the Fart Squad was now sitting on a dirt floor, with heavy metal shackles on their wrists and ankles.

Yes, they were imprisoned in a cold and dank dungeon for a thousand years, at least nine hundred of which would not be necessary.

Yes, they were quite possibly trapped in the year 1502, and would probably never see their parents again.

Yes, Tusheeburgh, Scotland, now had a tyrannical boy king whose only friends

were two giant slabs of human ham as dumb as rocks.

But Darren preferred to look on the bright side.

The Royal Butt Scratcher was no longer trapped inside a hunk of stone. That meant they had a much better chance of destroying it. If Darren got another shot at it, he wouldn't miss. They could still save Buttzville from the Itch. They could still complete the mission. Darren just needed to get his crew pumped again. They were looking pretty glum.

"Come on guys, *think*," he encouraged them. He was sticking to whispers so the guard at the gate couldn't hear them. "There's got to be a way out of this dungeon. Walter, what are you thinking?"

"I am thinking that turbo power burns gas far more quickly than standard power."

"Yeah, tell me something I don't know," Tina whispered.

"I didn't know that," Juan-Carlos admitted.

"Okay, so what's your point?" Darren asked.

"My point is this," Walter said. "Turbo Taco may give us turbo power, but it doesn't last nearly as long as our standard burrito power."

"Right," Darren said. "I'm with you so far. Keep going."

"Very well," Walter whispered. "If *I* have run out of power, then it can't be much longer before the three of you also run out of power.

What we need is the longer-lasting power of our traditional microwave burritos."

"Okay," Darren said, "but we're in medieval times. We're definitively not going to find any microwave burritos, so . . . ?"

"Precisely," Walter replied.

"That's it?" Darren said.

"You asked me what I was thinking," Walter said.

"Well, I'm thinking we're doomed," Juan-Carlos whispered. "I can't think of one single joke about sitting in a dungeon forever. There's nothing funny about that."

"For once, I agree with Juan," Tina said.

"Okay, then let's think it through again." Darren refused to be defeated. "If we're running out of power, and we don't have any burritos, then what can we do?"

"Drink more Turbo Taco?" Juan-Carlos suggested.

"But we already drank it all to get here," Darren said.

"No, but wait a second . . ." Tina finally started to perk up. "Remember what Mr. Buttz said before we left? He said the contents of the backpack were our only way back in time . . . *and* our only way home."

"*Right,*" Darren whispered. "If Turbo Taco sends you back in time, then there's got to be something in the backpack that sends you forward! Something that can get us home!"

"Indeed," Walter agreed. "Some kind of Reverse Turbo Taco."

"Taco Turbo!" Juan-Carlos cracked. "And he's *back,* ladies and gentlemen! I'd totally pat myself on the back for that one if I wasn't in shackles."

"Dudes," Darren whispered. "We've got a chance here. Tina, can you find a way to open the back . . . ?" Darren went silent when he looked at Tina's back. "Tina, where's the back-pack?"

"I hid it," Tina whispered.

"What'd you do *that* for?" Juan-Carlos moaned.

"Hel-*lo*," Tina replied, "Mr. Buttz was all '*do not lose* this backpack. Be *extremely* careful with it.' You think I was going to risk battling fifteen knights with that thing on my back? Anyone notice my perfect somersaults and cartwheels that were keeping us in the fight?"

"Yes."

"Yup."

"Indubitably."

"*Thank* you." Tina nodded.

"So . . . where did you hide it?" Darren asked.

"I found a loose stone behind the throne when the battle was going on.

It's hiding right under their noses."

"Okay, this is perfect," Darren said. "It's still the middle of the night, so King Harry and the twins won't be in the throne room; they'll be asleep. All we've got to do is get out of this dungeon and sneak back into that throne room. Then we get the backpack, drink the Reverse Turbo Taco, go turbo, destroy the Scratcher, save Buttzville, and fart our way back home!"

"Oh, is that *all* we've got to do?" Juan-Carlos whispered.

"Guys," Darren said, getting up on his knees. "We can *do* this. Walter may be out of gas, but *we're* not yet. I can get us out of these shackles. Tina can knock out the guard at the gate long enough for me to cut through one of the bars and grab his keys. We make a dash for the throne room, Juan distracts the knights with a time-bomb toot, and we're golden. What do you say? Are you in?"

"In."

"In."

"Indubitably."

"Okay!" Darren tried to pump his fist despite the shackles. "Now, Juan, hold out your wrists and stay *very* still."

The days of lightning butt were long gone. Darren had to bear down and push like he was giving birth to fart-uplets just to get a laser-thin butt torch going.

Still, slowly but surely, he managed to slice through all their shackles so they could sneak closer to the gate where the guard stood watch.

"What did I tell you?" Darren whispered. "Still not out of powers! Now, Tina, you just need to get close enough to the guard to knock him out."

"On it," Tina said.

She tiptoed up to the guard's back very carefully. Then she shut her eyes very tightly, like she was

SNIFF

trying to lay an egg. It was probably the least ladylike face Tina Heiney had ever allowed herself to make. But desperate times called for desperate measures.

She finally got her imaginary egg out and tiptoed back to the crew. Then they watched and waited for the guard to pass out. He began to sniff the air and crinkle his nose. Then he stumbled a bit, but regained his balance. Then he sniffed around again, stumbled again, and then *finally* fell.

"*Yes.*" Darren gave Tina a fist bump. "See that? Still not out of powers! I'm going in."

Darren ran to the bars and crouched down next to the laid-out guard. Just one more butt zap, and they were free. He crouched, aimed, and fired . . .

But nothing came out.

Crouch. Aim. Fire!

Nothing.

Darren's butt was as cold as a snowman's.

"Okay, now I'm out of powers."

And so, apparently, was Tina. The guard woke within twenty seconds of nodding out, and he opened his eyes to the sight of Darren's cold and powerless tush.

"ESCAPE!" the guard cried out, as he jumped back to his feet. "ESCAPE!"

A line of guards with torches came running down the dungeon's rickety, wooden stairs.

"These little wizards hath worked their evil magics again," the guard said, pointing at the Fart Squad.

But they weren't the Fart Squad anymore. And it was time for Darren to accept it. They were no more the Fart Squad than the B.O. twins were the Weight Watchers.

"Put them in the dungeon's dungeon,"

another guard ordered. "The king shall deal with them in the morning."

"There's a dungeon's dungeon?" Juan-Carlos squeaked as they hauled them all back to jail.

CHAPTER EIGHT

King Harry sat upon his golden throne with a huge turkey leg in one hand and the Royal Butt Scratcher in the other.

A butt scratcher that Darren was now totally powerless to destroy. He could only stand there in his shackles, lined up next to his best friends, watching Harry scratch and scratch to his heart's content.

Bertha and Oscar had been given wooden stools to sit on behind the throne. The chairs were far too small for their sizable derrieres, so they had to keep shifting from cheek to

cheek, trying to get comfortable. They also had not been given turkey legs, and Darren was pretty sure he could see actual drool dripping from the corner of Bertha's mouth, as she eyed Harry's turkey leg with burning resentment.

The giant knight and the bearded knight stood guard at the bottom of the marble stairs awaiting orders from their king.

In fact, everyone was just standing there while King Harry chewed his turkey and scratched his butt. Chew . . . scratch . . . scratch . . . chew. Until he finally decided to speak with his mouth still full of turkey.

"You," he said, pointing down at the bearded knight with his scratcher. "What's your name again?"

"Yes, my lord," he replied. "As I've told you before, I am Sir Angus MacClellan of the Tusheeburgh MacClellan clan."

"Yeah, I'm just gonna call you Beardy," Harry said between bites.

"As you wish, my lord."

"No *duh*, as I wish!"

"Of course, my lord."

"Big dude," he said, pointing his turkey leg at the giant knight. "Name."

"Yes, my lord. Sir Ewan MacKenna of the Tusheeburgh MacKenna clan."

"Yeah, not working for me," Harry said. "From now on, you're Sir Eats-a-Lot. Way easier to remember."

"A fine choice, my lord."

"Beardy!" Harry barked. "What are these losers doing back in my throne room? I thought I gave them a thousand years in the dungeon?"

"You did, my lord, but the

wizards attempted to escape the dungeon."

"Escape?" Harry stood up from his throne. "*Not cool,* dudes. Maybe I need to give you *two* thousand years! How would that be, huh?"

"That is why they've been brought before you, my lord," Beardy said. "So that you might choose their final punishment."

"Ugh, Harry, this is so boring!" Bertha blurted out. "I don't want to play Medieval Times anymore. I'm hungry and there's nothing to do here. I wanna go home and eat Taco Bell and play video games."

"Yeah, we want to go home, Number Two," Oscar said.

King Harry's cheeks grew flushed with rage. "How many times do I have to tell you? I am *not* Number Two! I'm Number One! I'm the king! This is *my* dream and you're going to stay in it for as long as I want. *I* decide when it's time to go. I decide all the punishments. I decide everything. Isn't that right, Beardy? Don't I decide everything? What I say goes, right?"

"Yes, of course, my lord."

"That's right." Harry seethed. "And you know what I say?" He threw his turkey leg to the ground and pointed his scepter at the Squad. "I say . . . Off with their heads!"

"Say *what*?" Juan-Carlos squawked. "Can he say that? He can't say that, right?"

"I just said it." Harry crossed his arms.

"I hate it here!" Bertha cried, standing up from her tiny chair. "I want to go home." Bertha ran down the stairs, bumping Darren like a linebacker on her way out of the throne room. Darren watched her lumber out of the room, and an idea suddenly struck him like a bolt of his own butt lightning.

Beardy stepped to the throne-room window and blew his ram's horn. "The king hath spoken! The wizards have been sentenced to death. Prepare the guillotine!"

"Prepare the . . . ? Did he just . . . ?" Juan-Carlos was having trouble breathing and finishing his sentences. "Okay, he did *not* just . . ."

"Juan, relax," Darren whispered. "I have a plan."

"Well, it better be a really, really good plan," Juan-Carlos whispered back.

Darren thought about it for a few more seconds. "It's . . . I mean, it's an *okay* plan."

Juan-Carlos's eyes widened with panic. "Just okay?"

"Guards!" Beardy called out. "Escort the prisoners to the guillotine!"

The guards came in and escorted the Squad out the door in their shackles. They were marched past Bertha who was sulking in the hall, and that's when Darren made the only play he had left.

He accidentally on purpose stumbled away from the guard and bumped himself into Bertha, braving the unbearable stink behind her ear to whisper to her.

"Backpack behind the throne," he whispered. "Bring it to me and I can get you home."

"Back off, freak!" Bertha barked, pushing Darren away.

"Keep moving, wizard!" Beardy warned, as the guard pulled Darren back in line.

"Wait, was that it?" Juan-Carlos whispered. "Whispering to Bertha? Was that the whole plan?"

"That was it," Darren said.

"Oh, dude." Juan sighed. "I'm a deadman."

CHAPTER NINE

The sunlight in the castle courtyard was blinding. Darren hadn't even realized how long it had been since he'd seen the actual sun. Nothing but caves, castles, and dungeons for the last twenty-four hours. Give or take five hundred years.

Unfortunately, the main thing reflecting all the sunlight was the giant steel blade of the guillotine. It was *so* much taller than it looked in the pictures. Probably because Darren had never seen it from the perspective of the dude who was about to be *beheaded*.

Come on, Bertha. You've got to come through.

All the Knights of Tushée came trotting into the vast courtyard on horseback, led by Beardy and Sir Eats-a-Lot (which, Darren had to admit, were pretty good names for them).

But riding in front of them all, of course, was their fearless leader and resident tyrannical dictator, Harry Buttz, Jr.—King of Tusheeburgh, world's worst horseback rider, and kid who still thought this was all a dream. The sight of him bouncing up and down on that big white horse, wielding a butt scratcher over his head like a sword, would have been hilarious under any other circumstance.

A butt scratcher. The Fart Squad was about to be executed . . . over a butt scratcher.

There it was, dangling right there in Harry's hand, just yards away. If only Darren had his *powers.*

You can do it, Bertha. You're more than just a slab of ham with legs. I know it.

Beardy trotted up next to the Squad and led them closer to the guillotine. Then he turned to Harry and the Knights of Tushée for his speech.

"Hear ye, hear ye! These ruthless bandit wizards have been convicted of—"

"Yeah, blah, blah, blah," Harry interrupted. "Let's just skip to the main event, Beardy. I don't want this dream to get boring."

"As you wish, my lord." Beardy turned back to the chain gang. "Which of you bandits shall be first?"

"I WILL!" they shouted in unison. They had all raised their hands at once.

"No *I* will," Tina said, jumping to the front of the line in her shackles.

"No way!" Juan-Carlos argued.

"Not happening," Darren added.

"Not within the realm of possibility." Walter jumped to the front of the line.

Juan-Carlos jumped in front of Walter, and Darren jumped in front of Juan-Carlos. But Tina still somehow made it to the front. Darren tried to stop her again, but she wasn't having it.

"Don't worry," she told him. "Your plan's gonna work."

Tina got into position and Darren's throat went bone-dry. He searched the whole court-yard, but there were no signs of Bertha *or* Oscar.

"Very well, then," Beardy said. "Guards! Release the blade on my mark. Three . . ."

"Dude." Juan-Carlos was darting his eyes all over the courtyard.

"Two . . ."

Darren started power-brainstorming for another way to stop the blade, including the use of his own arms, legs, and head. Walter was way ahead of him, inching closer and closer to the guillotine himself.

"One . . . Release the—!"

The sound of two whinnying horses suddenly rang out through the courtyard as all eyes turned to the gate.

Darren saw a sight he could never have imagined in his wildest dreams. . . .

The B.O. twins were each riding on horseback, racing across the vast courtyard at full Kentucky Derby speeds. They looked like lumbering slabs of ham when they walked, but when they rode . . . leaning deep into the gallop, fierce determination on their faces, they looked like two completely different people. They looked like the Lone Ranger and Tonto.

And Bertha was carrying the green backpack! She had it slung over her shoulder. Darren didn't know why she hadn't secured it on both shoulders, but a moment more, and he realized she had a very good reason.

It took a few moments for the Knights of Tushée to catch on, but once they realized the twins had joined the rebellion, a whole battalion began galloping in their direction. The knights had the instinct to go for the green backpack, but once they'd nearly reached Bertha, she flung the backpack over to Oscar!

They were playing a game of keep-away from the Knights of Tushée! Doubling their odds of getting the backpack to Darren. Were the twins secretly geniuses? Or were they just really, really mad about that turkey leg? Darren honestly didn't care, as long as they could fling him that backpack before the knights got to it.

The knights managed to corner Oscar, but Bertha caught the bag for the final goal run toward Darren. She was getting so close, he could taste it. They locked eyes and she cocked back the bag for the final toss . . .

But Sir Eats-a-Lot got to her first!

He reached for the bag and snatched it with his giant chain-mail glove, but Bertha wouldn't let go no matter what. The fight for the bag pulled them each off their horses, and they landed in the dirt, just flat-out wrestling for it. Bertha Scroggy vs. Sir Eats-a-Lot. It would have made millions for the WWE.

"Let go!" Bertha grunted.

"I shan't let go!" Sir Eats-a-Lot growled.

"You'll never take me alive, Knights of Tushie!" she hollered.

"It's pronounced Tu-*shay*!"

"Not in *my* house, it isn't!"

Darren wanted in on the fight so badly, but he was still shackled and fully guarded. He *needed* that backpack. . . .

But sheer size finally beat out dogged determination.

Sir Eats-a-Lot rose from the ground and raised the bag triumphantly, even though he had no idea what was in it.

"'Twas a very nice try!" Eats-a-Lot bellowed with a scornful laugh. "But no one defeats the Knights of Tushée!"

Darren was almost convinced that Eats-a-Lot was right. Maybe no one *could* defeat the Knights of Tushée? It seemed like the fight was over, and the bad guys had won. Until Bertha made the strangest noise. A yelp...? A cry...?

Or an amazingly high-pitched poot?

"Ugh!" Bertha groaned, wobbling around the courtyard in no particular direction.

"Ugh!" Oscar groaned from the other end of the yard where the knights were trying to hold him.

"I don't feel right," Bertha moaned, grabbing her sizable gut with both hands. "I feel like I'm having some . . . problems."

"Uh-huh," Oscar called out. "Problems. Big, big . . ."

Another inexplicable high-pitched sound came from Bertha's side of the yard, then from Oscar's. It was kind of like the sound of a jazz orchestra warming up, only it was excruciatingly painful to the ear, and it was mostly trombones.

"Oh, man, I got to let one rip!" Oscar cried.

"Ditto!" Bertha moaned.

And then . . . it happened. Whatever *it* was . . . it happened.

A sound that literally shook the ground. A sound that made everyone in the courtyard cover their ears and beg for mercy.

A sonic boom, made all the more powerful

because it was in *stereo*. Two Scroggy butts forming one stereo fart that shook Castle Buttz to its core. A sound that would later be described in certain lesser-known history books ... as the Devil's Trombone.

And the smell.

If pain had a smell ... it would be this.

The Fart Squad instinctively ducked

down and pinched their noses as the Devil's Trombone swept across the courtyard, sending every knight and every horse tumbling to the ground. Most important, it sent Sir Eats-a-Lot falling to the ground like a giant redwood, dropping the backpack right at Darren's feet.

Even with shackles on, he was able to grab the bag and zip it open, and sure enough, white smoke began pouring out. There *was* a second bottle of Turbo Taco! This one had a label with two forward triangles, like the fast-forward symbol on a video player. This was the way back home!

Darren popped the cork for a swig, but then he saw that the bottle was nearly empty.

"Oh no . . . ," he murmured, as the situation grew clearer. "Bertha! Did you drink this?"

"Uh-huh," Bertha groaned.

"Did you drink almost *all* of it?"

"I was *so* hungry," she said, "and it smelled like . . . Taco Bell."

"And farts," Oscar added. "Taco Bell and farts. Or Taco Bell farts? Mostly Taco Bell."

Of course the B.O. twins would have hardly noticed the foul stench of Turbo Taco. Their noses had been desensitized by years of their own foul stench.

"You *both* drank it?" Juan-Carlos asked.

"Uh-huh," they replied.

"And when precisely did you ingest it?" Walter asked, his face darkening with worry.

"Right before we got on the horses," Bertha said.

Darren could see Walter making the estimation in his head. "Perhaps ... two minutes ago ... ?"

"Oh my god," Darren breathed. "That only leaves them two minutes to make the jump, before ..."

"*Reverse Diarrhea.*" Juan-Carlos was visibly queasy just thinking about it, though he still wasn't quite sure what it meant. "But wait, no . . . because this bottle sends you *forward* in time, so . . . maybe not reverse diarrhea? Maybe just incredibly bad *forward* diarrhea?"

If the Devil's Trombone was any indication of what the twins could do on Turbo Taco, then Darren didn't even want to know what kind of diarrhea it might be, or how many acres of medieval Scotland it might cover. The simple fact was this:

The Fart Squad now had two minutes to

complete their mission. And Darren wasn't about to waste a second.

He lapped up a drop of Turbo Taco, hiked the bottle to Walter, and down the line it went like a live grenade until finally, at long last . . .

The Fart Squad was fully powered up again.

Not just fully powered. *Turbo* powered.

CHAPTER TEN

Two minutes to save Buttzville from the Itch. Two minutes to destroy the Scratcher, save the twins from some kind of nightmare diarrhea, and make the jump back home.

First things first. Time to lose the shackles. There was no time for keys, and definitely no time for laser precision. Darren bent over, tucked his wrists through his legs, and fart-blasted his handcuffs off. Then he went straight into a crouch and blasted the ankle cuffs.

"Fart Squad, line up, single file!" he ordered. "Get the hands up high. And dudes, this is gonna hurt."

"Do it!" Tina said, stretching to line her wrists up with Walter and Juan-Carlos.

Darren fired off a low-impact lightning bolt that melted their cuffs right off, and then he ducked down for the straight shot to melt off the ankle cuffs. He was finally getting the hang of his turbo-powered lightning butt.

The moment they were free, their eyes all zoomed to the exact same spot. Not that far off in the distance, there was a gold butt scratcher being waved wildly in the air by a little king who was searching desperately for a horse. His white horse had escaped to the Tusheeburgh Forest, scared off by the deafening squeal of the Devil's Trombone.

The Fart Squad didn't even have to speak. They knew what to do. Tina and Juan-Carlos approached by land, while Walter took to the sky, grabbing hold of Darren's hands and flying him high into the air.

They closed in on Harry like a hawk. But this wasn't about Harry. It had never been about Harry. They had come back in time for one reason, and one reason only.

"Can you lock on to the target from this height?" Walter shouted through the wind.

"You bet your turbo-powered butt, I can," Darren said. He closed one eye and lined up his butt cheeks with the Royal Butt Scratcher. But then in rode the Knights of Tushée, galloping right into his sights, ruining his clean line of fire.

"WE MUST PROTECT THE KING!" they cried.

Beardy galloped his way up to King Harry and swooped him up onto the saddle.

"Walter," Darren said. "I don't know about you. But I have had enough of these knights."

"We simply don't have time," Walter agreed.

"Hey, Beardy!" Darren shouted down to him. "Beardy!"

Beardy finally looked up at Darren. Sadly, he now answered to "Beardy."

"Leave the king alone, wizard!" Beardy warned.

"I don't care about the king! I just need the Scratcher!"

"You shall never get the Scratcher. Your magic doesn't frighten us. Nothing short of a full-grown, fire-breathing dragon can scare the Knights of Tushée!"

A smile cropped up in the corner of Darren's mouth. "Walter, can you fly ahead of them?"

"Easily, but we've got less than sixty seconds."

"They want a dragon?" Darren said. "Let's give 'em a dragon."

Walter smiled. "It's the least we can do."

They'd already learned what happened when you crossed Darren's turbo power with Walter's turbo power. They'd just never thought to do it on purpose.

Walter poured on the speed, pulling ahead of Beardy and his crew, and then Darren unloaded a full-powered lightning fart straight into Walter's fart stream.

While there probably weren't any official fart-lightning record books, Darren was pretty confident that he and Walter had just broken the record for the biggest lighted fart in history—breaking the record they'd set more than five hundred years in the future.

Much more important, they'd created the most epic fireball that any knight had ever seen. And then they created another. And another. And another. Beardy and his crew looked positively terrified.

Had the Knights of Tushée ever faced an actual fire-breathing dragon? Probably not. But would anyone believe them when they told the tales of the farting superheroes from the future who shot fire and lightning out of their butts? Probably not. And Darren didn't really care. He wasn't in it for the glory. All he cared about was that he finally heard the four words he'd been dying to hear since he came to Castle Buttz:

"Knights of Tushée . . . RETREAT!"

Beardy and all the rest of them took a turn so sharp that the Scratcher slipped from King Harry's hand.

"My scratcher!" he cried out, reaching for it and falling off the back of Beardy's horse.

The Scratcher rolled to a dead stop in the grass.

"Thirty seconds!" Walter told Darren. "Do you have a clean shot?"

Darren closed one eye and lined up his butt cheeks with the Scratcher. "I'm locked on! No, wait!"

King Harry leaped on top of the Scratcher to protect it. He'd already lost the Scratcher to Darren once, and he really didn't want to lose it again.

"Not this time!" Harry shouted up at Darren. "I'm not going to let you—*WHOA!*"

Harry was launched five feet off the ground before he landed with a thud, grimacing. But the grimace wasn't from the pain; it was from the smell. Juan-Carlos climbed out from a patch of bushes and gave Darren the thumbs-up as they soared by.

"Twenty-five seconds!"

They swung back around for one last try.

"No!" Harry stumbled his way back to the Scratcher in a fart daze. "I'm the King of Tusheeburgh and it's my scratcher. Because I'm Number—"

King Harry fell flat on his face, passed out cold.

Tina gave the thumbs-up, finally clearing the way for Darren's lightning. It was something that poor King Harry would simply never understand: teamwork.

"Twenty seconds!"

"I'm locked on," Darren said. "Firing!"

He squeezed out one truly thunder-ous bolt that blew the Scratcher into clouds of metal dust. And then he took a deep breath.

"Mission accomplished," he said. "Let's bring her in for a landing."

Walter and Darren landed just a few feet from where King Harry lay passed out like a baby. Tina and Juan-Carlos were doing their best to help the twins along, but it was not easy, given their giant, hamlike heft.

"Ten seconds and counting," Walter said.

"Everybody grab a finger," Tina said, pulling the twins into their circle.

The circle formed around Harry, and they all looked down at him for their last remaining seconds in the year 1502. They had clearly all had the same thought for those last few seconds, but Tina was the one to finally say it.

"Should we bring him back?"

"I'm fine either way," Bertha said.

"Don't worry about it," Juan-Carlos said. "The tailwind will take him back with us anyway. Wait . . ." He cracked his classic goofy smile. "*Tail*wind? Did we go this whole time and I never made a joke about the—?"

"Juan!" Tina interrupted him.

"What? Oh, right, sorry. I love this part..."

"Four, three, two..."

"PULL MY FINGER!"

CHAPTER ELEVEN

Darren woke up with his face in a bed of fresh-cut grass. A groundskeeper on a big lawn tractor buzzed by him at a peaceful, leisurely pace.

There were definitely no lawn tractors in medieval times.

Darren pushed himself up, took a good look around, and realized where they were.

"Dudes!" He quickly climbed to his feet. "We're not in Tusheeburgh, Scotland. We're in Buttzville Park!"

Tina sat up and dusted herself off as best she could. Then she studied the grounds-keeper as he drove away. Her face lit up with a huge smile of relief. "We *did* it," she said.

"I know," Darren agreed. "We made it back."

"No, not that," Tina said. "Look at the groundskeeper."

Juan took a good, long look. "What? He's not doing anything."

"Precisely," Walter said with a celebratory grin.

And then it clicked for Darren. What the groundskeeper was not doing was scratching his butt.

The Squad and the B.O. twins all stood up and started looking for more proof.

There were two kids playing Frisbee in the park, not scratching their butts. And a family having a picnic, not scratching their butts. And two whole touch-football teams not scratching their butts.

"What about you guys?" Darren asked. "Anybody feeling itchy at all?"

"Nothing." Juan-Carlos grinned.

Bertha, Oscar, Walter, and Tina all agreed. They were itch-free.

"My butt itches," Harry mumbled, as he woke from a sound sleep. "Whoa . . . where am I?"

"You're in Buttzville Park," Bertha told him.

"I must have been playing in the park and fallen asleep. . . ." Harry rubbed his eyes. "I had the same dream I always have."

"Which dream is that?" Darren asked, shaking his head.

"The one where I get to be the king," Harry said. "Only this one was *way* weirder. This time it didn't feel like a dream at all. It

Scratch
Scratch
scratch

felt like a place." He looked up at the twins and the Fart Squad. "And you and you and you and you were there."

"Oh boy." Tina sighed. "He thinks he's in *The Wizard of Oz* again."

Juan-Carlos crouched down next to Harry. "Tell you what, Junior. Forget *The Wizard of Oz*. How about if you get to be the *Wizard of Itch*? How does that sound?"

"Do I get to have a Golden Butt Scratcher?" Harry asked.

"Golden Butt Scratcher?" Tina shrugged her shoulders. "There's no such thing as a Golden Butt Scratcher. It doesn't exist." She winked at the Squad, as she smiled proudly.

It was true. There had been no Golden Butt Scratcher since the year 1502. Because the Fart Squad had changed history.

Harry Buttz II had an itchy butt. Buttzville did not. And Fart Squad's noxious scents had made the world safe again.

THE END

BLAST OFF WITH . . .

HARPER
An Imprint of HarperCollinsPublishers

www.harpercollinschildrens.com